The True Story of Tabby and Her Family

by

Adele Hooker

Pictures by Thomas Bunker

Softcover 9781633825796
eBook 9781633826403
PUBLISHED BY AMERICA STAR BOOKS, LLLP
www.americastarbooks.com

Frederick, Maryland

PREFACE

I know animals don't talk in our language.
But you know, our pets hear us
and feel us all the time.
And I think they understand way more
than we think they do!

Our Tabby Cat was so smart!
I'm going to pretend
that she can talk like you and I do.
And if she could, this is the story
she would tell you.

Hello Friend!
My name is Tabby.
I'm a lucky cat!
I have a wonderful family and a wonderful home.
I love everyone and everyone loves me.

My lady's name is Adele. I call her "Mama."
Brother's name is Grant, and Sister's name is Mary.
Papa's name is Sam.

Grant and Mary love to hold me and pet me.
They tease me too!
That's how we play.
My Lady holds me on her lap a lot.
I like that.

They give me good food to eat.
Sometimes I even get food
under the table when they are eating.
That's a "No-No".
But Grant does it anyway.

I'm a special Cat!
I get to sleep with Mary in her bunk-bed.
It's yummy cozy!
I snuggle up to her and keep her warm.

Grant's bunk is on top. He can be naughty.
Sometimes he throws things on us
from up there.
That makes us mad!
Mary hollers out,
"Mama, Grant's throwing things on us!"
Mama comes in and scolds Grant
and he stops... sometimes.

My Lady has a pet chicken.
Her name is Biddy.
I love Biddy. We're friends!
Sometimes I eat her food
when my Lady gives her scraps.
Biddy doesn't care.
She shares.

We have a dog, too. Blackie is his name.
Blackie never chases me! But he chases Biddy-
hen.
Mama makes him stop.
She teaches us to be kind to each other
so we can live in peace together.
It's a lot more fun that way!

Each one of us is different and that's ok.
God made us that way.
My Lady said so.

I'm a very pretty Cat.
I have bright green eyes and long beautiful
hair.
And I never get fat.
BUT....

One day I started getting bigger...
and bigger ... *and bigger.*
I got real big and very fat.
My lady said,
"Papa! Tabby is going to have babies!"

Then she told Grant and Mary.
"Tabby is going to have babies!"
They got real excited!
"When? When?" they cried.
They could hardly wait.
I could hardly wait, too.
I was going to be a mommy!

I could feel the babies
moving around in my tummy
as they got bigger and bigger *and bigger!*

Finally one day
I knew the babies wanted out of my tummy.
I went to my Lady and meowed ….
REAL loud!
She saw my tummy wriggle and said,
"Oh Tabby!
You're ready to have your babies…. NOW!
I'll make a bed for you!"

At first she put me in a box with a blanket.
It was nice and soft, but….
It was a BOX!
I didn't want to have my babies in a BOX!
I wanted to have them where I slept,
on Mary's soft, cozy bed.
So I jumped out of the box
and up on Mary's bed!

"Oh Tabby!" Mama said.
"Of course you don't want to be in that box!
You deserve to have your babies
on the nice soft bed."
So she put a rubber sheet and a blanket
on the bed… just for me.

But then she surprised me.
She walked right out of the room!
I didn't want to be alone. I was scared!
So I followed her into the kitchen
and meowed REAL LOUD at her.

"What is it Tabby?"
I meowed again, trying to tell her
I wanted her to follow me.
She seemed to understand because
she followed me back to the bedroom
and put me on the bed.

But then Mama did it again!
She walked out of the room!
"Doesn't she get it?" I thought.
"She's supposed to stay with me!
I don't want to have my babies alone!"

Now I was *really* scared!
So I went out and meowed at her *AGAIN*...
Only this time I practically *screamed* at her!
She jumped!

"OH TABBY!" She said, as she picked me up
and carried me to the bedroom.
"You don't want to be alone, do you?!
You're scared!"

Mama laid me on the bed
and started petting me gently.
"You haven't done this before Tabby,
and it might be hard for you."

"Maybe you think you won't be able to do it.
But God made it so that
you *can* do it.
And I'll stay with you to comfort you.
Maybe that will give you courage.
I'll pray for you, too".
She whispered her prayer very quietly.

"Dear God," she said,
"Please help our Sweet Tabby
have her kittens without any trouble.
Strengthen her for this **Big Job.**
Thank you. Amen."

And pretty soon…
A Great Big Pain came
and I just had to *push!*
I pushed and pushed
and…. ***Plop*** !
A baby kitty fell out of me!

My Lady ran and told the children,
"Come quick!
Tabby's having her babies!"
They hurried in and stood around my bed.
Blackie and Biddy came running too.
They all wanted to see how I gave birth
to my babies.

I kept on pushing. I couldn't help it.
My body just did it... and
Plop! Plop!
Two more kitties fell out of me.

"Good Job, Tabby!" the children cried.
"You have three beautiful babies!"

Everyone was proud of me,
even the Daddy.
Grant said I was brave and strong!
Mary thought it was wonderful
the way I had my babies.
Mama said, "Tabby, I am SO proud of you!
You did a great job!
You are a wonderful pet
and a wonderful mother."

I was proud.
But I was tired.
It's a Big Job to have babies!
I just wanted to sleep.
So I laid on the bed and let my babies
nibble at my tummy to nurse.

They crawled all over me,
those beautiful little kittens of mine.
But I slept anyway!
Because THAT was the biggest job
I'd ever done in my whole life!

THE END